Sister

Books by Eloise Greenfield

MARY McLEOD BETHUNE

PAUL ROBESON

ROSA PARKS

SISTER

UNDER THE SUNDAY TREE

Sister

By Eloise Greenfield
Drawings by Moneta Barnett

HarperCollins*Publishers*

J
G

Designed by HARRIET BANNER

Manufactured in the United States of America

Library of Congress Cataloging in Publication Data
Greenfield, Eloise.
    Sister.
    SUMMARY: After her father dies a young black girl watches her sister withdraw from her and her mother.
    [1. Family life—Fiction]   I. Barnett, Moneta, illus.
II. Title.
PZ7.G845Si   [Fic]   73-22182
ISBN 0-690-00497-4

8   9   10

For my father
Weston W. Little, Sr.
who scuffled to feed us
and still found time
to bounce us on his knee

and

for my mother
Lessie B. Little
Her life is a gentle Black joy/love song.

oh children think about the
good times

—Lucille Clifton
Good Times

Sister

"How you doing, Doretha?"

That's what Lonnie would say to her from the stage.

"Lonnie and the Liberations!" Doretha whispered to herself, reading from the ticket in her hand. She couldn't stop smiling. She sat down on the edge of her bed. Then she got up again and just stood there looking at nothing, still smiling.

"Sister," her mother called from downstairs, "come on down and eat dinner with me."

"Okay, I'm coming," Doretha said.

But she sat back down on the bed and looked at the free ticket she had gotten from Mr. Nelson at the recreation center. She rubbed her thumb across it, thinking about its magic. Tomorrow night it would take her into another world, through the gates of the outdoor theater, to see Lonnie and the Liberations. Instead of looking at their flat, still pictures in a magazine, she would be sitting right there looking at the real them. She might get near Lonnie, might even be able to stick out her hand and touch him. Touch him!

All of a sudden the joy exploded like cherry bombs inside her. She threw herself into the middle of the bed, bouncing and laughing loud, kicking her feet in the air like a little kid, instead of like thirteen. Then she lay still, the craziness gone. She closed her eyes and let herself slide into the daydream she had been making up ever since she got the ticket.

Lonnie would fall in love with her. He wouldn't care that she was still straight and skinny or that she was a year behind in school. Somehow, even in the dark, crowded theater, he would see the love in her eyes and he would say, "How you doing, Doretha?" over the mike in a cool warm way, without her even telling him her name. And that would be their beginning.

"Come on up here with me."

His voice was pulling her up, up, out of her seat. She was walking, almost floating, down the long aisle. All her friends were watching, and she didn't know why she felt so proud when she never liked for people to stare at her.

Music was coming from somewhere, and then the Liberations were singing, and Lonnie was singing just to her, drawing her down the aisle. She reached the bottom of the stage and he spun around in a circle, still singing, and threw out his hand to help her up the steps. The audience was going wild, clapping and stomping and cheering for their love. She could only look at him as he held her hand and sang . . .

Bam!

The slamming of the door downstairs jerked Doretha out of her daydream. It was her sister. She heard her mother walk from the kitchen to the front room. She sat up and tried to make her mind a wall to protect her from the argument that was about to start.

"Alberta, do you *have* to slam that door like that?" Mrs. Freeman said.

"I'm sorry," Alberta said. But she didn't sound sorry.

"I told you a hundred times not to . . ."

"I said I was sorry, Mama! What you want me to say?"

"Who you think you talking to, Alberta?" Mrs. Freeman said. "Just who you think you talking to? You raise your voice at me again, I'll slap you winding."

There was a long silence. Doretha could imagine her mother's soft eyes, soft brown heart face, tight and bitter now that Alberta was home. But she knew her mother would never hit anybody, much less slap her own daughter hard enough to send her winding around and around.

"You look for a job today?" Mrs. Freeman asked.

"Yeah."

"Well?"

"I didn't get one," Alberta said, and Doretha could hear the worry in her sister's voice even with fourteen steps between them.

"I told you if you left school you had to get a job," Mrs. Freeman said. "And I don't care if it is summer now, you still not going to just sit around here . . ."

"I been looking for a job for two months."

"You had no business leaving school. Sixteen years old, hanging around the streets all day with those hoodlums . . ."

Doretha's mind-wall crumbled. She got up and closed the bedroom door, then went over to look out the open window. Dark summer clouds were growing in the sky, and she should have been setting out the buckets to catch the rain that would drip through the leaks in the roof. But she waited.

She leaned on the window sill and tried to slide back into her daydream, but closing the door hadn't shut out what was going on downstairs. She knew what they were saying. She knew it was the same as the time before. And the time before that. And all the other times. Her mother would be holding her slender body still, except for her hands opening and closing in the pockets of her housedress. Alberta would be sighing and shifting her slight weight in cut-off jeans from one side to the other, her long, thin face longer and her halter top exposing more collarbone than she wanted.

They not hoodlums, they my friends.

I've done all I can to make you happy, Alberta, I don't know what else to do.

I have to get out sometimes, Mama.

Heading for trouble, Alberta, trouble, Alberta, trouble . . .

The first slow raindrops struck Doretha's hand and she closed the window. She stood watching the balls of water hit the window and break.

"Don't you ever want to get away from here?" she had asked her mother a few days ago.

"Sometimes I do, Sister."

"You know what I wish, Mama? I wish I could just stand up and throw my arms out hard, real hard, and knock that falling-down roof all the way to New York. And that old, beat-up refrigerator. And school."

She longed to *breathe,* to inhale with her whole body new air. She wanted to feel the way Alberta looked when she danced. When Alberta danced, she was up high where coolness caressed the nostrils, she was free. She would close her eyes tight, and swing her arms and legs and shoulders and hips to the beat of the music. But when the music ended and she opened her eyes, she would leave the house, slamming the door behind her.

"I wish people would stop saying I look like Alberta," she had said to her mother that day.

"Don't you think Alberta's pretty?"

"Yes, but . . ."

She couldn't say it, not even to her mother. But she wanted to. She wanted to say, "I'm so scared, Mama. Everybody keeps saying I'm just like Alberta, walk like her, talk like her, look like her. And I know sometimes I feel like her. And I'm scared. Maybe by the time I'm old as she is, I'll stay out late every night or not come home at all. Maybe I'll make you cry, Mama, and put worry lines in your forehead. Maybe I'll even have a fingernail scar like hers curving down the side of my face."

But worse, worst of all, and she knew she could never say it, maybe she would have eyes that way, way back, deep inside, cried without tears.

It was raining harder now, and Doretha started to worry about tomorrow. They might have to call off the show, and she wouldn't get to see Lonnie after all. Nothing important would happen to her, and she wouldn't have anything to write in her Doretha Book. It would be just another summer night.

"Sister!" her mother called. "Can you get the buckets?"

"Okay, I'll get them," Doretha answered.

She was still holding her ticket and she slid it under the box of colored pencils on her side of the dresser before she ran downstairs.

In the front room, Mrs. Freeman was sitting in the stuffed chair beside the small upright piano. Her Afro was mashed out of shape against the chair back and her eyes were closed. Alberta stood at the door, holding the knob and glaring at the back of her mother's head.

"Hi, Alberta," Doretha said.

She didn't expect an answer and she didn't get one. Alberta didn't even look her way, and when Doretha got back from the basement with the buckets, her sister had gone.

Doretha took the buckets upstairs and set one in her mother's bedroom under the yellowed circle on the ceiling. The other one she set in the middle of the bathroom floor just in time to catch the first drop. She washed her hands and went back downstairs.

Her mother opened her eyes. "If Mr. Johnson doesn't get those leaks fixed by the first of the month," she said, "I'm not giving him another penny of rent."

"You eat yet?" Doretha asked.

"I was waiting for you, but I think I'll go lie down awhile." She stood up. "They think people are horses over there at that laundry. And soon as I get home good, here comes Alberta slamming in like she owns the house."

"I fixed chili," Doretha said.

"I know, and it looks real good, too. I'll eat some later." Mrs. Freeman started up the steps. "You go ahead, honey, don't wait for me."

Doretha ate and washed dishes and put the food away. Her mother wouldn't come back down tonight. She sat on the floor in the front room and watched television until she got sleepy. When she got in bed, she could still hear the rain hitting the window. She looked over at Alberta's empty bed, and the last thought she had before she went to sleep was, "Please, please, *please* don't be raining tomorrow."

When she woke up in the morning, Alberta's bed was still neat. But the rain had slackened, and early in the afternoon it stopped. By the time the slow hours had passed into late evening and Doretha could leave for the recreation center, the sun had dried the sidewalk in front of her house. She stopped at the house three doors down.

"Shirl, you ready?" she asked the girl who answered the door.

"Yeah," Shirl said. "See you later, Ma!" she called, closing the door without looking back. Her yellow eyelids matched her dress, but looked strange with her full-cheeked baby face.

"How you like my eyes?" she asked Doretha. "I stayed upstairs until you came so Ma wouldn't see."

"They look good," Doretha said, "if you like lemons for eyes."

Shirl laughed. "I thought they looked pretty hip, myself. I looked at that chick in the mirror, and I told her, 'Girl, you are baaad.' "

When they got to the center, their friends were already crowding on the bus. They were laughing and pushing, and somehow Doretha and Shirl got separated. Thomas took the seat beside her, and Shirl made a face over his head as she passed. Doretha wished that Coley, sitting across the aisle with Lynn, could somehow change places with Thomas. She knew it was a stupid wish. Most of the time now, Coley pretended he didn't even see her.

Mr. Nelson got on last and sat in the front seat. As soon as the driver started the bus, Bernard, sitting in the wide back seat, turned his transistor radio up loud. Lynn whispered something in Coley's ear that made him laugh, and they got up to dance in the narrow aisle.

"Hey, you kids sit down!" the driver yelled at them. "Where you think you at?"

His close haircut made him look out of place on the bus. All the boys wore Afros, and even Mr. Nelson had a small one.

"That's right, Mr. Cleanhead," Bernard said. "That's right, you straighten them out." He turned the radio up louder, and two more couples got up to dance.

Everybody laughed except Thomas, who looked nervous.

Mr. Nelson turned around in his seat. "Okay, okay, that's enough," he said. "Turn that radio down some, Bernard."

He spoke calmly, but they knew he meant it. All the couples danced back to their seats. Doretha watched Coley and Lynn laughing and whispering, and felt bad. It was dark now, and she could see them and their reflections at the same time. But when the bus pulled up in Rock Creek Park, her stomach went *zip, zip,* and she forgot all about them. Shirl caught up with her as they got off the bus.

"I feel funny," Doretha said, patting her stomach.

"Me, too," Shirl said.

Their seats were near the back, but Doretha didn't care. She looked around the huge theater.

"Oh, wow!" Shirl said. "Look at that, Doretha. Look at the trees."

"Tree walls," Doretha said.

"Yeah, walls. And look at the roof!"

The sky was the roof, black sky sprinkled with stars. Doretha felt her *self* moving away from Shirl, away from everybody, while her body sat still. When the show started, she didn't listen to the girl singer or the comedian. She only heard the crickets chirping in the woods. She was waiting. For Lonnie.

Screams. Four dashikis flashing. Drums beating. Lonnie! Lonnie at the mike. "Why, why, why did you you go, did you leave. . . ." Three pairs of arms swing up, back, out, bodies swaying—step forward, step back, turn around, clap! turn around, clap! Sweet, sweet guitar. "It's a brand new wor-orld. . . ." Lights spinning orange, blue, purple, spinning purple. Purple! Shirl singing softly. Voices whining—"Sing to me Lonnie baby, awww *shucks* now, oh my Lord." Screams. Exploding hands. Seats and people shrinking, sliding away, Lonnie singing for her. To her. "Ooh-ooh, babay, ba-bay, ba-a-baaa," going higher—"aaaa"—shrieks from far away coming in waves—"aaaa"—higher, stretching, stretching—strange, she felt strange—"aaay" sliding down to its finish. Endless scream of joy and pain—hers? Oh, Lonnie, Lonnie.

After the show, Doretha didn't feel like talking. She stared out the bus window all the way back to the recreation center. She wanted to hold onto the feeling and not let the magic go. She wanted to hold onto it forever.

"Hey," Shirl said when they were walking home. "It's me, your friend Lemon Eyes, remember?"

Doretha smiled and said, "I know, I know."

Shirl opened the black iron gate to her front yard. "Well, see you. You think you'll be talking again by tomorrow?"

"Maybe," Doretha said. She laughed with part of herself, still holding the magic close. When she reached her door, she waved at Shirl, who was waiting on her porch, and Shirl waved back. Doretha unlocked the door.

"That you, Sister?" her mother asked, coming to the doorway of the kitchen.

Her voice sounded as if it were caught in a pocket of her throat, her eyes were red, and Doretha remembered—Alberta was gone again. Now the magic had gone, too. Doretha closed the door.

"She's not back?" she asked.

Mrs. Freeman shook her head. She went back into the kitchen and opened the door of the refrigerator. "I was trying to figure out dinner for tomorrow," she said. "I guess you better fix this stew beef. Not much of it, but see if we have enough potatoes to stretch it."

Doretha checked the bin under the sink. "There's enough," she said. She went over to her mother. "She always comes back, Mama."

Mrs. Freeman fought to keep her mouth from trembling. "Maybe this will be the time, Sister," she said, "maybe this will be the time she won't come back. She could be lying out there dead somewhere right now."

"But she's not," Doretha said, trying to sound as if she believed what she was saying. "She's not, Mama."

Her mother looked at her as if she suddenly remembered that Doretha was only thirteen. "Of course not, honey," she said. She put her arm around Doretha and kissed her cheek. "I'm letting my imagination run wild." She tried to laugh. "I forgot to ask you about the show."

"It was okay." She wasn't ready to talk about it yet, any more than her mother was ready to listen. "You going to bed now?"

Mrs. Freeman smoothed her hands across the red plastic covering the table. "In a few minutes. I'm going to straighten up down here a little first."

"Okay." Doretha watched her mother for a second. She felt much older than thirteen. "Good night, Mama."

"Good night, Sister. You go on to sleep now. I'll tell Alberta to wake you up when she comes in."

When Doretha got in bed, she had with her a very old, very worn notebook, her Doretha Book. It belonged to her, and she was in it. Each page was a special memory, a special time, written in a special color.

She sat with her knees propped up, her pillow behind her and her book hugged to her chest. She closed her eyes and thought about Lonnie. No matter how much she wanted it to be true, she knew he hadn't really been singing to her. But the music had been real, and the night, and the new air she had breathed. And for just a little while, she had been free.

She opened her book and turned the pages until she reached a clean one. From the box on the dresser, she took a deep purple pencil. Very slowly, in her best handwriting, and large enough to cover the whole page, she wrote, "Me, age 13. Tree-walls, sky-roof, Lonnie —Love."

Then she flipped the pages back to the beginning, watching the colors of her life go by. She made a bet with herself that by the time she had finished going through the whole book, from beginning to end, and remembering, the front door would slam and Alberta would be home again.

The first page was written in black. It said, "Me, age 9. My Doretha Book—Memories."

Doretha was bored sitting there on the sofa with her white-casted leg stretched out. She could hear her friends outside jumping rope.

> *Mama, Mama, don't cry, don't cry,*
> *I jumped all the way to the clear blue sky,*
> *I touched the sun, but I ain't gonna die,*
> *Oh, Mama, Mama, don't cry, don't cry.*

Just two days ago she had been doing the same thing, jumping in and out of the rope and reaching up to touch the sun, when she landed on a rock, twisted her foot, and broke her ankle. Now here she was, stuck during the Easter holidays. She was tired of television, tired of playing jacks, tired of sitting on the porch watching her friends play. Her sister had gone out. And inside the cast, her leg itched.

"No sense in you sitting there with your mouth stuck out, Sister," her mother said. She moved the dustcloth over the dark brown wood of the second-hand piano. "Alberta's been entertaining you for two whole days, and she's got a right to go out with her friends sometime."

Doretha didn't answer. She sat slumped against the arm of the sofa. She usually enjoyed watching her mother dust the piano very carefully as if it had feelings and too hard a touch would make it cry, but today it seemed dumb. She heard a key in the door and stuck her lips out more.

"Hey, how my girls doing?" Her father was home, tall and neat in khaki pants, his short beard hiding the top of his turtleneck shirt.

"Hi, Cle." His wife left the piano and met him at the door. She reached up and touched her lips to his, then rubbed her face against his beard. "Tired?"

He shrugged and threw his jacket on the chair. "Uh-oh," he said, looking at Doretha. "Thelma, what you been doing to my baby?"

"I didn't do a thing to her," Mrs. Freeman said. She laughed, and all three of her dimples dotted her face. Even the one Doretha called a high dimple, at the top of her right cheekbone. "Alberta went to the movies with Brenda, and your baby's feeling sorry for herself."

Doretha's father came over to her. "She sure does look mean," he said. "I bet she wouldn't laugh now if a joke walked right up and tickled her in the gut." He tickled her side and the laughter fell out of her. "Hey, that's better. Tell you what. While I'm getting some of this dust off me, I'll try to think of something we can do, me and you and Mama. But it won't be going for a ride, I tell you that right now. I parked so many cars today, I don't want to see nothing on wheels."

In a little while he was back, carrying a cardboard beer box.

"What's that, Daddy?" Doretha asked.

"My junk box. Stuff I had when I was in high school. Everything in here is sixteen or seventeen years old. Been saving it just for the time you'd try to beat up a rock with your big toe." He set the box on the coffee table and went to the kitchen to get two chairs. "Put that broom down, Thelma, and come on. We need you in here, too. Okay, Sister, you pick out what you want to look at and I'll tell you all about it."

Doretha took her time going through the things in the box, looking at pictures of her father and his friends in front of the three-story red brick building, a birthday card from a girl named Joyce, a magazine clipping of Miles Davis blowing his trumpet and one of Jackie Robinson.

And then she saw the frayed corner of the loose-leaf notebook sticking through. She lifted it out. It was large and black, and at the corners gray cardboard showed through the worn covering. On the inside of the front cover was written, "Clemont Freeman, Cardozo High School." The book was filled with yellowed lined paper, most of it unused. It looked a hundred years old to Doretha.

"Daddy!" she said. "Can I have this?"

"You don't want that, Sister," Mr. Freeman said. "It's probably got paper lice all over it."

"You can spray it, can't you?"

"Now, Sister," her mother said, "Cle wants to keep that. What in the world you want it for?"

"I don't know. Yet. But I'll think of something. Please, Daddy? You can take out the paper you wrote on."

"Well ..."

"You spoiling her rotten," her mother said. "You know that, don't you?"

"Uh-huh," her father said. He leaned the chair

back on two legs. "I spoil all the women in my house. Man gives his wife a piano and she plays it with two fingers, what you call that?"

Mrs. Freeman looked at the piano and back at her husband, and smiled. None of her dimples showed, but her eyes were tender.

Doretha didn't have any idea what she would do with the book. But it was so old and ugly and beautiful that she had to have it. She took it to bed with her every night, and in a few days she knew how she would use it.

"Mama," she said one morning, "how you spell memories?"

Coley walked, springing up and down on his
tennis-shoed pigeon toes, around the long picnic table,
looking at the food. "Your Aunt Mae made a applecake, didn't she?" he asked.

"Uh-huh," Doretha said.

"She make one every year," Shirl said, "don't she,
Doretha?" Her face was round, and her shorts had
slid down under her stomach.

Coley looked at each cake, partly hidden under
wax paper. "I hope it's this big one," he said. He

climbed up on the gray wooden bench attached to the table and spread his arms like a preacher giving benediction. "I'm the king of the picnic," he announced.

"No, you not," Doretha said. "My father's the king. It's *his* birthday."

"Hey, look," Coley said, pointing away from the table, "you can see good up here."

Doretha and Shirl climbed up on the bench. Doretha turned slowly all the way around and saw her father and some of the others over in the field playing ball, Alberta and Brenda sitting in the swings, playing the transistor radio and telling secrets, and Uncle Harold sleeping against a tree near the women playing cards. She turned around again, faster, to bring all the people closer together.

"I know what!" she said. "Let's go visit everybody."

Shirl jumped down. "Yeah," she said. "And when we finish, it'll be time to sing to your father."

"And then we can eat," Coley said. He jumped as far as he could and slipped in the dirt.

"Run, Daddy, run!" Doretha yelled.

Mr. Freeman touched first base, ran around second, and came back just before the ball came in from the outfield. Aunt Mae got a hit and went to first base. And Uncle Floyd knocked the ball over Mr.

Walker's head, and they all came running in, Doretha's father fast-striding, Aunt Mae flying in red pants, and Uncle Floyd leaning forward, pushing his big shoulders ahead of his knees. They came in laughing and slapping hands.

"What's the score?" Coley asked.

"Hey, Walker," Uncle Floyd yelled, "they want to know the score."

"Can't hear you," Mr. Walker yelled back, laughing.

Mr. Freeman said, "Thirteen to nothing, Coley. They haven't even been up, and we not about to let them get up neither." He sat down on the grass to wait for his next turn. "Sister, you want to bring us some sodas out the ice chest?"

Doretha, Shirl, and Coley raced toward the picnic table.

"And a couple of beers," Uncle Floyd called after them. "And don't shake them up."

"Hi," Shirl said.

"Hey, Brenda," Alberta said, "you know these little kids?" She stood up, letting the swing dangle, and Coley jumped in.

"Uh-uh," Brenda said. She shook her head and her long metal earrings jingled. "I never seen them before. But one of them must be your twin sister. She got on plaid jeans and a green shirt just like yours, and she got a short 'fro like yours, too."

Doretha laughed and pinched her sister's arm. "I know," she said. "You just don't want us to come over here 'cause you telling secrets."

"They talking about boys," Shirl said.

"How you know?" Brenda asked.

" 'Cause that's all you talk about," Shirl said, "boys, all the time, boys."

"Hey," Coley said. "Look at me." He was standing up and swinging high.

"Look at Coley!" Doretha said.

Alberta punched Brenda with her elbow. "I think somebody else likes boys besides us," she said.

Doretha pinched Alberta again, and kept pinching her. "I don't, I don't," she said.

"Okay, Sister, okay," Alberta said, laughing and running away. "I take it back, I take it back."

"Mr. Harold goes to sleep every year," Coley said.

"Just leave him right alone," Aunt Flossie said. "The man drives one hundred and fifty miles every year to get here, and he needs his rest." She fanned herself with the cards in her hand, and her huge arm shook. "But before this time next year, I'll have my license and I'll be able to help him out some."

"Aunt Flossie," Doretha said.

"Yes, Sister?"

Doretha backed off a little from the card table so her great-aunt couldn't reach her. "You say that every year, too."

"All I got to say is it's a good thing I give myself to the church last month, or you'd get it, Sister." She kept her face straight, but Doretha laughed.

"Your play, Flossie," Doretha's mother said.

"Yeah, Flossie," Mrs. Walker said. "You going to play cards or run your mouth?"

"I'm doing both, just like I always do," Aunt Flossie said. "Church ain't changed me that much."

"You ain't supposed to be playing cards no way, are you?" Miss Pauline asked.

"This my last game, Pauline. I promised the Lord, just one more game to celebrate Cle's birthday, and He said it was all right long as I . . . Sister, why you standing there looking in my face like you don't believe a word I'm saying?" She fanned herself again. "And just look at you. You get any more like Alberta, I won't be able to tell you apart. Remember when you were little and you used to slide around in Alberta's shoes, and if we didn't call you Alberta, you got mad as fire? I wouldn't do it just to . . ."

"Flossie, will you play!"

"You holding up the game, Flossie!"

"Just put down a card, any card!"

"*Happy birthday to you, happy birthday to you.*"

It sounded like a thousand voices.

"*Happy birthday dear Cleee, happy birthday to you.*"

"How o-old are youuuuu?" It was Aunt Flossie's sanctified soprano.

"Hold it," Mr. Freeman said. "You might as well hold it right there, 'cause I'm not about to tell my age."

"Come on, everybody," Mrs. Freeman said. "Help yourself to the food, and after we eat, Cle can open his presents."

"No, sir!" Uncle Floyd said. "Cle ain't opening nothing until he tells us how old he is."

Mr. Freeman laughed and took the plate of food his wife handed him.

Alberta poured herself a cup of lemonade.

Doretha's daddy laughed, he laughed, he laughed a funny, jerky laugh that twisted his face. His fingers let go of the paper plate and the fried chicken legs slid down, down, through the air and *plopped* in the dirt. His fist beat against his chest.

Doretha's mama leaned forward, reaching.

Doretha's daddy rocked, he rocked backward, then forward and down, down, through the air until his face *plopped* in the dirt.

Uncle Floyd turned Doretha's daddy over.

Doretha's daddy stared at the sun without blinking.

Doretha's mama fell down on her knees, bending over Doretha's daddy and screaming his name. Doretha's daddy didn't answer, he wouldn't answer, he wouldn't answer.

Aunt Mae hugged Doretha's mama. Doretha's mama hugged Doretha's daddy. Alberta cried out of tune.

The man put a cover over Doretha's daddy, hiding the dirt on his face.

The ambulance driver stole Doretha's daddy, stole Doretha's daddy, stole Doretha's daddy.

Doretha's daddy was gone.

Alberta picked up her cup and tasted her lemonade. "It's warm," she said. Her eyes filled with tears and she started to gasp.

Doretha started to cry, too, and Aunt Flossie's cushiony arms came around them both.

"Cry on Aunt Flossie," she said in a low, trembling voice. "Cry on your Aunt Flossie."

Doretha cried hard. She didn't understand today. They had all been so happy. She had turned around twice in a circle and covered herself with their happiness.

And now, the lemonade was warm, the chicken legs lay in the dust, and her daddy was dead.

Doretha came out of the kitchen with her mouth stuffed full of oatmeal cookies.

"Where's Alberta?" she mumbled.

"Hmmm?" Her mother was reading the paper and didn't look up.

"Mama. Where's Alberta?" Doretha repeated. "I been home a long time."

Her mother looked up. "Sister, just look at your mouth!" she said. "What time is it, anyway?"

"Way after three."

"Well, it's the first day of school. She and Brenda are probably poking along somewhere." Mrs Freeman laughed. "I just hope she hurries up and gets here before you have a fit. Your sister can't go to the bathroom without you asking where she is." She turned back to the paper.

"Mama." It was Alberta, standing in the open doorway. She was breathing hard and sweat was standout on her forehead. "Mama . . ."

"Alberta!" Mrs. Freeman dropped the newspaper and rushed to the door. "You're sick!" She felt Alberta's forehead and neck with the back of her hand. "Come on, honey, let's go upstairs. Close the door for me, Sister."

Doretha closed the door and followed her mother and Alberta upstairs. Alberta leaned against her mother.

"Brenda's gone, Mama," Alberta said. Her voice shook.

"Shhh," Mrs. Freeman said. "Don't talk right now. Let me get you in bed first and then you tell me about it."

She took off Alberta's skirt and blouse and helped her get in bed. She pulled the summer blanket up and sat on the bed beside her, rubbing her hand. "Now, tell me what happened," she said.

"Brenda didn't come to school," Alberta said, "so I went over her house just now, and Mr. Miles said she and Mrs. Miles went to Georgia."

Doretha stood beside her mother, watching the throbbing in Alberta's neck. She didn't understand why her sister was so upset about Brenda's visit to Georgia. "When they coming back?" she asked.

"They never coming back," Alberta said. "Mr. Miles said they never coming back. They took all their clothes and everything."

"How come?" Doretha asked.

"Sister, don't ask so many questions," her mother said.

"Why didn't Brenda tell me, Mama?" Alberta asked. "I just saw her the other day and she didn't say she was moving. Remember the day we rode our bikes? Remember, Sister?"

Doretha remembered that she had wanted to go.

"Mama," Alberta said, "why don't people tell you when they going away? Daddy didn't, and Brenda didn't either. Why don't they, Mama?"

Doretha thought she saw her mother draw in, but she wasn't sure. "Sit up, honey,' Mrs. Freeman said. "Here, put your head on my shoulder." She put her arms around Alberta. "You know your father wanted to stay with you, don't you, Alberta? And so did

Brenda. But they had to go. And they couldn't tell you 'cause they didn't know themselves. But you'll be all right. Sister loves you, and I love you, and all your other friends, and we're here . . ."

Mrs. Freeman held Alberta and talked quietly, and Alberta was silent for so long that Doretha almost thought her sister was asleep, except that now and then a shudder would pass across the blanket.

The next day, and the next few days, Alberta went to school sad and came home sad, and Doretha missed her. Then her mother got a job at the towel laundry, and Doretha missed her. She got home first every day and opened the door with her key, and the house seemed emptier than when her mother went downtown or to Aunt Mae's.

The day Brenda's letter came, Alberta started to smile again, and Doretha was happy until she realized that something about her sister wasn't the same. She tried to remember exactly how Alberta used to look when she laughed, and how her voice used to sound when they talked across the room at night. But she couldn't. Something was lost. Something important was lost. And she didn't know what it was.

One Saturday when Doretha was dusting her room, she heard her mother downstairs making up a song. Mrs. Freeman would hum a note and find it on the piano, then put it with the notes that had come before.

Doretha went downstairs and stood beside the piano. "That's a sad song, Mama," she said.

"Is it?" Mrs. Freeman kept on playing.

"Is it about Daddy?" Doretha asked.

"Uh-huh."

"Why you have to play a sad song? I don't like it." Her voice was rising.

Mrs. Freeman stopped playing and looked at Doretha. "Then go upstairs and close the door, Sister."

Doretha didn't go all the way upstairs. She sat on the steps above her mother's head, hoping she would notice and feel sorry for her. But her mother was playing again.

"My stomach hurts," Doretha whined after a few minutes.

Mrs. Freeman sighed and dropped her hands in her lap. She closed her eyes and sat for a moment, and Doretha felt guilty watching her mother sit like that.

Finally, her mother opened her eyes. "Sister," she said, talking very slow, "I need this song. Right now, I need this song. I can't be Mama for a little while. I got to be just me, just Thelma. Just for a little while. And after that, I'll be stronger and I can help you. You understand?"

Doretha looked at the floor.

"I want you to go on up to your room now," her mother said. "Go find something to do and I'll be up in a few minutes, and we'll talk. Go ahead, now."

The piano didn't start right away, but by the time Doretha had taken her jacks out of the dresser drawer, she heard it again. She sat on the floor and practiced picking up her eightses and nineses until her mother came up.

"You upset about Alberta, aren't you?" her mother said, not really asking. She sat down on Doretha's bed. "I was hoping you wouldn't notice, but I should've known you wouldn't miss a thing."

"Why doesn't she like us anymore?"

"She likes us, honey. Alberta loves us. She's just closed herself up 'cause she's scared. She's scared that if she lets herself love us too much, we might leave her."

"But we wouldn't!" Doretha said.

"Not if we could help it, Sister," her mother said. "Not if we could any way help it."

That night after Doretha went to bed, she looked across the room at her sister's back. Maybe her mother would have to go away sometime, she thought, but she wouldn't. No matter what. Not even to die.

"Alberta," she said.

Alberta didn't move.

"Alberta, I won't never go away. I promise. I won't never, never leave you."

Alberta moved her arm. But she didn't answer.

"**M**ama said you don't never write, Grandpa,"
Doretha said. She let go of the handle of the ice-
cream churn and wriggled her arm before she started
turning it again. "She told me not to forget to ask
you about your knee."

Her grandfather sat across from her at the round
maple kitchen table, taking clippings from a large
yellow envelope and pasting them in his Willie Mays
scrapbook. "It hurt right much, nowadays, Sister," he
said. "That Arthur's the meanest man I ever saw." He
rubbed his knee and laughed.

Doretha looked at him. "Who's Arthur?" she asked.

"Arthur Rytus. Ain't you never heard of him? He ever get after you, Sister, run your behind off!" Grandpa leaned his head back and laughed loud, bringing a vein line down his wide, dark forehead.

Just looking at her grandfather's face, taken over by laughter, made Doretha giggle. She looked at him and at the big country kitchen, and through the window at the snow-covered North Carolina fields. "I'm glad Uncle Floyd let me come with him," she said. She lifted the lid from the churn and looked in. "How long does it take?" she asked, putting the lid on again.

"It take a pretty good while," Grandpa said. "But just wait'll you taste that cream. You won't never eat store-bought no more."

Doretha turned the handle harder and felt a squeezing pain inside her arm.

"Grandpa?" she said.

"Hmmm?" He brushed a thin layer of paste on the back of a picture.

"How can you laugh when you hurting real bad?"

"Folks most always hurting somewhere, Sister. Feelings get hurt. Bodies get hurt. You don't laugh when you hurting, you won't hardly ever laugh at all.

Can't let pain beat you down, you know." He patted his knee. "Every day I take this old piece-a knee and wrap it up in a hot towel, damn near burn it off. I straighten it out and then I bend it and I keep on doing it with old mean Arthur Rytus in there scraping around on the nerves with a rake. And when I finish, most times it still hurt. So then I laugh at it. That's the way you got to do pain, laugh at it, all the same time fighting like hell." He placed the picture carefully in the book and rubbed his hand across it. "Your mama ever tell you about your great-great-grandpa?"

"My great-great-grandpa?" The sound of the words excited her.

"My grandpa," her grandfather said. "I didn't never see him, but heard about him plenty times from my mama. I told Thelma about him when she was a little girl. Told Alberta, too, when she was near about old as you are now. Tell you what. By time your grandma and Floyd get back from town, that cream ought to be ready and we'll dish us up some, and then I'll tell you all about him." He laughed and shook his head. "Grandpa Jack."

"Grandpa Jack was born back in slavery time over in Edgecombe County, about sixty miles from here.

His mama come from Guinea, way over there in Africa, when she was a baby. White folks stole her and her mama, put 'em on a boat and brought 'em here to be slaves.

"Grandpa Jack didn't remember nothing about his mama, 'cause by time he was old enough to know anything, she'd been sold off somewhere. All he knowed was what old Aunt Rilla told him about everybody being crammed in together so close coming over on the boat they couldn't hardly breathe, and folks dying. And about his mama going out in them fields every morning before day and working past evening dark. And how she wouldn't let them white folks see her cry, and wouldn't smile at 'em neither.

" 'Your mama was proud,' Aunt Rilla used to tell him, 'looked on herself.'

"Well, when Grandpa Jack was about ten years old, the folks what imagined they owned him—'cause can't nobody never really own nobody else, Sister, you remember that—well, them folks put him in charge of the fireplace, putting wood on it and keeping it lit all day, and putting ashes on it at night to make it go down.

"And he had to sleep right there on that stone hearth, with nothing under him but rags, so he could wake up before day and build the fire back up, and by time them folks put their precious feet on the floor, it'd be all nice and warm. Poor little fella used to wake up in the middle of the night so cold he be just shivering and aching all over. Got whipped more than once, too, for sleeping too late in the morning. Make me mad as a mule, Sister, just to talk about it.

"Well, when he got bigger, he got a new job. They learned him how to make shoes, and he made shoes for everybody on the place. And after the slaves was freed, he moved into a little cabin way out from there with some other black folks, did some carpentering and shoemaking, and after some years he built hisself a little place of his own. Made a fair living.

"He was a fine-looking man. Not too tall, but big shoulders and hands, like your Uncle Floyd. Proud, too, like his mama. Looked on hisself. After while, he got married and had seven children. But he didn't never forget them nights lying there on that cold hearth, and them whippings. Every time it crossed his mind, he got mad.

"'I'll wade in blood up to my knees, *up to my knees,* if any white man ever lay a hand on my children!'

"Used to say that all the time, and his voice would rumble like one of them big dump trucks going over a wooden bridge, and folks all over the county knowed he meant it.

"Well, one day this white preacher come round

wanting some shoes, and Grandpa Jack's second boy was watching 'em and listening to 'em talk the way smart children do. Learning about the world. Well, the preacher, he got mad. Said the boy ought not to be looking up, ought to be looking down at the ground.

" 'I'll teach you to look up in a white man's face,' the preacher said. Then he spit right in the boy's face. Sure did. Hawked it up and spit it right in his face.

"Well, Grandpa balled up his giant fist and rammed it in the preacher's jaw, knocked him down, and went for the rifle he kept hid in the house. But by time he come back, the preacher was gone.

"Grandpa knowed he would be back with his friends, though, so he kissed his wife and all his children, even the biggest boy, and took his rifle down by the black folks' church and waited for 'em. And when he seen 'em coming, he started shooting. Laughing and shooting, laughing and shooting. Got the preacher first and got two more before they shot him down. They left him laying there, but late that night his wife and his friends went and got him. They said he was still smiling when they buried him.

"White folks said he was a crazy nigger, but black folks knowed he was fighting the pain of all them memories of losing his mama and slaving and getting whipped and seeing that mess in his boy's face and leaving his wife and children. Fighting the pain, yes, sir! Fighting it and laughing at it."

"Your mama laugh much nowadays, Sister?"
"Not with her high dimple, Grandpa."
"Well, when you get back up home, you tell her I said don't never forget she's the great-granddaughter of Grandpa Jack. You tell her that, hear?"

Doretha stopped suddenly at the door of the classroom, and Shirl stepped on her heel.

"Don't stand there looking stupid," the woman
said. "Come in and take your seats."

The woman sitting at Miss Booker's desk spoke
slowly, giving each syllable an equal amount of time.
She was smiling and shaking her head, jarring the
rooster wrinkles on her skinny neck. The smile didn't
move when she talked, but stayed spread across her
mouth like a threat. Her stiff, light-colored wig looked
hideous against her brown skin.

"Look like straw," Shirl whispered to Doretha after they had sat down.

Doretha sensed something familiar about the woman, something unpleasant, but she couldn't think about it right now. Coley was already in his seat and now she knew why he hadn't waited for them this morning. He was leaning over, talking to Karen.

"Everyone sit down," the woman said, "and stop talking." The room quieted down immediately, and Doretha wasn't surprised. Even Bernard would know this wasn't a substitute to play with.

"I'm Mrs. Garner," the woman continued, "and I will be your teacher for these last three months until school closes."

"Where Miss Booker?" Willie James asked.

"Where'sss Miss Booker," Mrs. Garner corrected him. "Miss Booker is minding her business, and we will do the same. Now, when I call your name, please raise your hand." She looked down at the open book on her desk. "Larry Adams."

"Yeah." Larry lifted his fingers from his desk and let them drop again.

Mrs. Garner smiled at him, and after a moment he raised his hand.

"Geneva Armstead ..."

Everything was going wrong, Doretha thought. Coley. And now Miss Booker. She didn't think she could pass without the extra help Miss Booker had been giving her.

"... Freeman."

Doretha raised her hand, and Mrs. Garner leaned forward and stared at her as if she were examining her face for pus bumps.

"Do you have an older sister, Doretha?" she asked.

"Yes."

"Yes," Mrs. Garner said. "Same sweet little face, same innocent-looking eyes. I always remember the students who give me trouble. Roberta, isn't it?"

"*Al*berta," Doretha said.

"Alberta, yes. I taught her in sixth grade, too." Mrs. Garner sat back and smiled broadly at Doretha. "Well, Doretha," she said, "I certainly hope you learn faster than your sister."

Doretha looked hard at the stick people somebody had scratched on her desk. She heard a snicker. It sounded like Karen. She remembered Mrs. Garner now. She had come to the house to explain why Alberta was going to fail. She had been fat then, and her wig was red.

In the afternoon, they took turns going to the board to multiply fractions. Doretha waited nervously, dreading the moment when Mrs. Garner would call on her. When it was her turn, she concentrated on writing the problem neatly, then began to work it.

"What in the world are you doing, Doretha?" Mrs. Garner asked.

"I was trying ..."

"You're not trying very hard. You certainly don't need that three. You're doing the problem all wrong. Erase it."

Doretha erased the problem.

Mrs. Garner smiled at the class. "She erased the whole thing," she said.

"You told me ..."

"Doretha, I told you to erase the three. The *three,* Doretha." She grinned and shook her head. "Just sit down, child, before you trip and fall over your own stupidity."

Doretha felt the inside of her stomach tremble with hatred, and she forgot to be embarrassed. The wrinkles on Mrs. Garner's neck were moving and making her feel sick.

"I don't care!" she yelled. "I don't care what you say!" She slammed the chalk against the wall.

"I knew it," Mrs. Garner said calmly. "I knew the minute I saw that face that you would make trouble."

"I hate you, I hate you, I hate your ugly face!" Doretha screamed. But the anger was leaving her body with her words, and she realized the class was staring at her. She stood there, silent, while everybody looked.

Mrs. Garner let her stand there in the quiet. Then

she said, "If you've finished your little tantrum, you may go back to your seat. And don't come to school tomorrow without your mother. Larry, will you pick up that chalk, please?"

Doretha brought her lips together tightly and pushed her head up in the air. She tried to walk the way Alberta did when she hid her feelings. She walked slow, slow, loose. As if she didn't care about anything.

Or anybody.

Doretha didn't know just what it was, but there was something different about Mrs. Anderson today. When Doretha went up on the porch, Mrs. Anderson was sitting kind of squeezed into the green metal chair, like she was every Sunday afternoon in the fall. She had on the same bulky-knit sweater, and her short gray hair was brushed back and bobby-pinned at her ears.

Maybe her plump, brown hands were lying extra still in her lap, or maybe her eyes were looking too far

47 ·

away. Whatever it was made Doretha pause before disturbing her.

"Mrs. Anderson?"

"Yes? Oh, hello, Doretha, I didn't see you come up. How are you today?"

"Fine. Mama said Mr. Anderson wanted to see me."

"He certainly does. Go right on in. I think he's in the living room."

Mr. Anderson met Doretha at the door. "I thought I heard you, Doretha," he said. He was cheerful, smiling behind his rimless glasses and under his thin, mixed gray mustache, but the house seemed to have taken on Mrs. Anderson's mood. He led her into the front room. "Sit right down there in the big chair. I have a present for you."

"But my birthday's not until February," Doretha said.

"Now, could I forget when your birthday is?" Mr. Anderson said. He pushed at the sides of his glasses. "The way Cle was bragging the day you were born? But this is something I want you to have now." He slid a long black leather case from behind the sofa, opened it and took out the silver instrument. He put it in Doretha's lap.

"Your flute?" she said. She held the flute with one hand to keep it from rolling off her lap.

"I want you to have it," Mr. Anderson said. He stood with his back swayed like a man with a big stomach, but he had hardly any. "Remember when you were little and you used to sit in that chair and listen to me play? And you called me Mr. Flute, remember? I might not have been the best musician in the world, but I'll bet I had the best audience. You and Mrs. Anderson."

Doretha was too surprised to think of being glad. She couldn't imagine Mr. Anderson without his flute. "You giving me your flute?"

"I have to go away in a little while, and I can't take many things with me. I know you'll take good care of it."

"I will!" Doretha said. Now she felt the excitement of the cool metal in her hands. "But why you *giving* it to me? You need it when you get back."

"I won't be coming back," Mr. Anderson said. "I can't come back this time."

"Oh."

"Here, let me put it back in the case for you, so you can take it home. And if your mother says it's all right, I'll give you a lesson every Saturday until I go away."

"I know Mama'll say okay," Doretha said. "Can we start this Saturday?"

"This Saturday is fine. Oh, I almost forgot." He

picked up a bag from the coffee table and handed her the record album that was in it. "Here's something I bought especially for you." On the cover was a dark, slender-faced girl, set back in deep brown shadows, holding a blue-silver flute. "That's Bobbi Humphrey. Beautiful girl like you, not too much older than you, either. Plays black music." He looked out the window. "If I could turn the clock back, that's the kind I'd play, too."

Doretha stood up. Through the window she saw Mrs. Anderson sitting just the way she had left her. "Is Mrs. Anderson sick?" she asked.

"No, she's worried. She's worried about my trip. She was always with me when I traveled before, and I'll be going alone this time. But I'll be all right. I'll be all right."

Going home, Doretha carried the flute up in her arms, instead of by the handle. She would take care of her flute the way her mother took care of the piano. She would love it as much as she loved Mr. Anderson.

He hadn't told her very much about his trip. She wondered when he was leaving. And where he was going all by himself. And why he couldn't ever come back.

And then she knew.

She held the flute tighter, but she kept walking

and didn't cry. When she got near home, she saw her mother watching her from the porch, frowning. Doretha smiled a little and waved, and the frown disappeared.

"How you like it?"

Mrs. Freeman laid the dress out on the bed. Its loud geometric designs stood out against the solid blue bedspread.

"It's dynamite," Doretha said. "Try it on."

"I was hoping you'd ask me that," her mother said, laughing. "It'll be filthy by the time me and Turner get to the cabaret. This is the third time I had it on today." She took off the terrycloth robe she was wearing and slipped the dress over her head. Doretha helped her pull it down. "I went by Mae's after I got off work to pick it up, and you know I had to try it on for her. And when I stopped by Pauline's a little while ago to borrow her long coat, I tried it on for her."

Doretha zipped the dress up the back, and her mother held her arms out and modeled back and forth. The long dress with its colorful circles and squares and triangles brought out the curves in her slender figure. "You can't tell me I don't look good, Sister," she said. "I can't wait to see Turner's face. I wish I could've bought those sandals I saw on Georgia Avenue, but I'm not going to worry about that. Look at these sleeves. Mae really did her stuff on this one, didn't she? I told her, too, and you know what she said? She said, 'Nothing's too good for my baby sister when she's in love.' I told her she must be crazy. She knows I'm not in love. I told her . . ."

"Mama, you know what?" Doretha said.

"What?" Mrs. Freeman stopped walking.

"That was a gooey song you were making up on the piano last night."

"What you mean?"

"You know what I mean," Doretha said, teasing. "It sounded like a love song to me."

"Now, Sister . . ."

"I like Turner, Mama," Doretha said, "I like him a lot."

"You do? You sure? You real sure?"

"I'm real sure."

Her mother smiled, but her eyes were wet. "Well, then," she said, "if you like him, I like him, too."

Doretha just looked at her mother.

"Okay, you're right," Mrs. Freeman said. "I love him."

"He's nice," Doretha said. "He's not like Daddy, but he's ..."

"He's just Turner. And I love him, and you like him, and Mae likes him, and ... you think Alberta likes him a little bit?"

"She likes him," Doretha said. She didn't want her mother to think about Alberta right now. "You going to dance when you go out tonight?"

"Sure, I'm going to dance."

"Let me see you."

Mrs. Freeman moved her feet and shook her shoulders, making gentle gestures in the air with her hands and humming as she danced. She held her slim hips almost still.

Doretha started laughing. "You can't just move the top, you got to move the bottom, too. Anyway, that's old, Mama, that's real old."

Her mother looked up in the air and kept dancing. "Just don't you worry about it." She tried to keep humming, but her laughter got in the way. Her high dimple flickered and set.

Doretha was laughing partly at her mother's dancing, but mostly because she felt so good. They were laughing so hard they didn't hear the downstairs door open.

But they heard it close.

Mrs. Freeman stopped dancing. "Unzip my dress, Sister. Hurry up."

By the time Alberta reached the top step, Doretha had laid the dress on the bed and her mother was tying the belt of her robe around her waist. Doretha was surprised to see that Alberta was smiling.

"What was so funny?" Alberta asked.

"Mama was . . ."

"We were just acting the fool," Mrs. Freeman said quickly.

Alberta's smile faded. "What's the big secret?" she asked. "Why can't I know?"

"You make fun of everything, Alberta," Mrs. Freeman said. "You make me feel so . . . silly."

"Well, I don't mean to."

"I guess you don't, honey." Mrs. Freeman patted her face. "Where you been all evening?"

Doretha sat down on the bed and sighed loudly.

Alberta said, "Nowhere. Me and Renee were just walking around."

"I wish you wouldn't stay out so late," Mrs. Freeman said. "I asked you over and over not to stay out after dark unless you at somebody's house. And Sister, there's no sense in you sitting there looking disgusted."

"You don't have to talk about that now, Mama," Doretha said. "We were having fun." She fingered her mother's dress beside her.

Alberta looked at the dress. "You going out?"

Mrs. Freeman nodded. "With Turner," she said. She waited, and Alberta shrugged. Mrs. Freeman picked up her dress, took it to the closet and hung it up. "Well, I guess I'll go soak for a while. If Turner calls before I get out, ask him what time he's picking me up."

She looked at Alberta, but Alberta was silent. And in a few minutes Doretha heard the water running in the bathtub.

"Sister, get the cards," Alberta said then. "Let's play some tonk."

Doretha pretended not to be surprised. She got the cards from her dresser drawer, and they sat on Alberta's bed. Doretha shuffled and dealt. She felt good again, not laughing good, but old times good, sister good. She watched Alberta without looking directly at her.

You in a good mood. Say it.

"You in a good mood tonight," Doretha said.

Alberta plucked a card from the deck and put it in her hand. "You know how cute Laverne thinks she is? Well, she went with me and Renee to this party in Southeast, and we told her we'd pay her bus fare back. And then we sneaked out and left her there." Alberta laughed. "Renee's crazy. She said she hopes Laverne'll be walking from now until next Juvember." She laid a card on the bed.

Be careful, Doretha.

"Shirl heard Renee got locked up for stealing earrings at Harrison's." Doretha plucked a card and put it down.

Alberta picked it up. "Watch out, Sister, I'm going to beat," she said, laughing. She spread three eights. "Yeah, Renee did get busted, but her mother went down and got her out until the trial."

"Aren't you scared you'll get in trouble going around with her?"

"Now you sound just like Mama."

Be careful!

Doretha spread. "I just wish you'd stay home more, Alberta. I don't never see you."

"You wait, Sister, just wait until you fifteen. You won't be sitting up under Mama all the time. Hanging around here, blowing on that flute. You can't play it no way, and Mama won't never be able to pay for lessons. But you just wait. After while you'll want to get out and have some fun. And you going to do it, too. Just like me."

You a lie!

"You a lie! I won't never be like you!"

Alberta's eyes blinked once, then veiled over. She opened her hand and let the cards fall on the bed. "Go to hell," she said.

Doretha watched her go to the closet and take out a dress. She knew what she had done. She had killed her sister. Alberta was still alive, but Doretha's sister was dead. She had killed her with words. She didn't know what had made her say it. She only knew that she couldn't take it back, and that now nothing would ever be the way it had been a long time ago for her and Alberta.

The phone rang downstairs. Alberta was taking off her shirt, and neither one of them moved to get it.

"You going to sit there and let it ring?" Alberta said. "It might be Mama's precious boyfriend."

It wasn't. It was a woman.

"Turner there, sugar?" the woman asked Doretha. "No."

"Well, this is his wife, sugar. I been out of town. But I got some real interesting letters from some of my friends, so I thought I better come home and see what was happening. Now, if I see Turner first, I'll tell him you all don't want to be bothered no more. But if you see him first, you just tell him his wife is home. Okay, *sugar?*"

The phone clicked and Doretha put the receiver down. She heard the bathroom door open.

"Was that Turner?" her mother called. "I thought I heard the phone." She ran downstairs in her robe. The hot water had steamed her hair close, and her bare feet left damp prints on the floor. "Was that . . . what's the matter?"

"She was looking for Turner."

"Who was it?"

"She said she was his wife."

"His wife?" Mrs. Freeman laughed, then stopped. "His wife? Turner doesn't have no wife. Don't look so upset, Sister. You know Turner doesn't . . . I bet it was Pauline. Did it sound like Pauline?" She looked at Doretha but didn't wait for an answer. "Some people carry a joke too far. I ought to call her back and tell her that wasn't funny. No, he might try to call. I better stay off the phone. I'll . . . I'll just sit right here and wait for him to call. That's what I'll do."

She sat down on the sofa, and in a few minutes

Alberta came down. And they sat there, the mother in the middle, slowly opening and closing her hands, and her daughters. Waiting.

Doretha tried to find Turner with her mind, find him at home beside the phone or in a drugstore pay booth, and will him to dial the seven numbers that would make their phone ring.

After a long while her mother said, "He's not going to call." And then, "I wonder why Turner did that, I wonder why he did that." And finally, "I sure do miss Cle." She started to cry softly, and the sobs that shook her shook Alberta as she held onto her mother.

"Mama, don't cry," Doretha was saying over and over. "Don't cry, Mama."

And she was crying, too.

ME, AGE 13. AUNT MAE'S APPLECAKE—DYNAMITE!

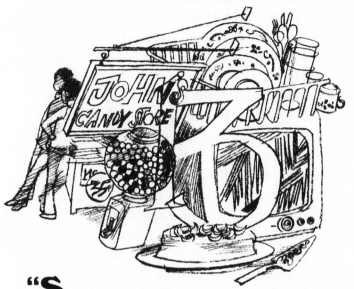

"**S**ister! You deaf?" Aunt Mae called from the front room.

"I didn't hear you, Aunt Mae," Doretha called back. She folded the dishtowel and hung it over the rack.

"I guess not, the way you singing and carrying on. I said how long you going to take, washing those little bit of dishes?" She lowered her voice when she saw Doretha come into the room. "About time. The movie's coming on, and I hate to watch T.V. by my-

61 ·

self." She turned several knobs on the television set. "How the devil you get this thing to stand still?"

Doretha made a fist and banged on the top of the set. The picture slid around once more and stopped. "I'm glad you came over," she said. "Mama's working late today."

"Thelma's going to let those folks at the laundry work her to death, you know that?" Aunt Mae sat down in the stuffed chair and crossed her legs. "Hey, why don't you run down to the corner and get us some potato chips? Keep me from biting my nails down to the quick while I'm watching the movie. It's a murder mystery." She got her shoulder bag from the sofa and gave Doretha some change.

Doretha went to the closet for her coat. She put it on, tied a triangular scarf around her neck to hide the worn collar, opened the front door, and stopped suddenly.

"Why you just standing there?" Aunt Mae asked.

Doretha closed the door quietly. "They over there on Bernard's front," she said.

"Who?" Aunt Mae went to the window and lifted the yellow nylon curtain.

"The boys," Doretha said. "Aunt Mae! Don't let them see you looking!"

Aunt Mae dropped the curtain and stepped back.

She put her hands on her hips. "Now, Sister," she said, "I know you not scared of boys."

"I'm not scared of them, I just don't like to walk by them. Coley's over there, and he acts so . . . so funny. Most of the time he doesn't even speak unless he's by himself."

"He knows you crazy about him, that's why," Aunt Mae said. She leaned her head to one side and widened her large eyes at Doretha. "And I guess when he feels like opening his mouth, you talk to him?"

Doretha didn't answer. She started taking her coat off.

"Put that coat right back on, Sister!"

"But, Aunt Mae . . ."

"I mean it. Put it on right now." She pulled the coat up on Doretha's shoulders. "I never heard anything so simple in all my life. Can't go out your own house unless somebody goes out there first to see if the street's clear of boys. Now, all you got to do is like this. Watch me now." She walked across the room with a little bounce, making her accordion-pleated skirt swing. She was the size Doretha wanted to be, not really slim, but not fat either. "How you doing?" she said to the floor lamp standing beside the sofa. She waved her arm and kept walking. "Now you do it," she told Doretha.

"I can't walk like you," Doretha said.

"Well, walk the way you walk, just don't draw all up like something's going to bite you."

Doretha felt silly, but she tried to imitate her aunt. She walked across the room and waved her arm. "How you doing?" she said.

"That's good, that's good," Aunt Mae said. "Now do it again and say it louder."

After the fourth time, Aunt Mae told her she was ready. "I'll be right here behind the curtain, watching," she said.

"They still there?" Doretha asked.

"Yeah, they still there, and if they weren't, I'd go find them. Thelma let you sit around here daydreaming all the time, you won't never learn how to deal."

Doretha put her hand on the doorknob, and a sudden thought made her panic. "What about when I'm coming back?" she asked.

"When you coming back, think about how good those potato chips going to be, and don't even look over there unless somebody says something to you."

When she got outside, Doretha didn't look across the street right away. She was concentrating on how she was walking. Not too fast, not too slow. She didn't hear a break in their laughing and talking, but when she turned her head to look at them, the boys were looking at her.

"How you doing?" she said with a quick wave.

"Hey Doretha, hey baby." Walter and Larry spoke, and Bernard gave her the black salute. But Coley stood still and cool with his hands in his pockets and his feet turned in just slightly. Doretha turned her head away.

At the store, she bought the potato chips from Mr. Carter and started back. She looked straight ahead and walked in rhythm with her thoughts. "Potato chips, potato chips." As soon as she passed the boys, she started to grin. Aunt Mae was laughing when she opened the door for her, and they leaned on it and closed it together.

"I did it, I did it!" Doretha said, laughing and hugging her aunt.

Aunt Mae put her hands on her hips. "You bet your Aunt Mae's applecake you did it. And the next time that sometimey, jive joker tries to speak to you, you tell him where to go and what to do when he gets there. Now, come on watch the movie. You missed one murder already."

The neatly hand-lettered sign on the door of the basement apartment said, "NDUGU NA NDADA. KNOCK HARD," and Doretha did. The man who opened it was a lot more than six feet tall, and his loose-fitting African robe didn't hide his muscular energy.

"Come in, sister," he said. "I'm Brother Juba." He shook her hand.

Doretha stepped inside. "I saw your poster on the telegraph pole in front of my school," she said, "and I came to see if I wanted to join."

"Good," the big man said. "I'm glad you came. What's your name?"

"Doretha Freeman."

"All right, Sister Doretha, I'll take you back to Sister Shani, and she'll tell you all about our school."

He took her through the front room, where a group of small children sat in a circle on the floor, counting painted sticks. All the girls wore long wraparound skirts, and the boys wore dashikis.

Sister Shani sat crocheting in the room that had once been a bedroom. Her African dress hung from the shoulders, and her hair was cornrowed from back to front, forming a curlicued frame for her face. She didn't look too many years older than Alberta. Doretha sat down in the chair beside her.

"Bet you don't know what Ndugu na Ndada means," Sister Shani said after Brother Juba had introduced them and left.

Doretha shook her head. "But I know it's African," she said.

"That's right, it's Swahili. It means brothers and sisters. We thought it was a good name for the school 'cause that's who we here for. The brothers and the sisters." She continued to crochet as she talked. "We just started taking teen-agers today, you know. You the first one to come. And if you like it, maybe some of your friends will come too. Now let me tell you what the school's about. First of all, we about freedom. Black freedom. And for that we got to learn all we can, right?"

Doretha nodded. She liked Sister Shani already, liked the way she just started talking as if they had known each other for a long time. She liked the room too. It was small and didn't look like a classroom. They were sitting at a table with several chairs around it, and over by the window was a sewing machine. The walls were decorated with pictures of African people and a large map of Africa.

"Okay," Sister Shani continued, "so here we try to teach everything we need to know to get freedom and to keep it. We been working with the little children for a few months now, but we hardly had enough space even for them in the old place." She held up the wide ruffle she was making, looked at it, and put it back in her lap. "Then, last week the brother who's buying this building told us he had a vacancy in the basement we could use for free. Now that's what I call a for-real brother. Told us to come on in and stay, at least until the bank that lent him the money to buy it finds out and starts bugging him."

The children in the other room were singing and clapping out several different rhythms that ran together, and Doretha found herself trying to figure them out. "You teach reading?" she asked. "The poster said we could get extra help if we needed it."

"We sure do," Sister Shani said. "We got to know how to read. How else we going to know what's going on in the world? We teach history and math, too. And sewing. You get to make yourself a long dress. And we teach the history of the way black people in this country talk, how it's a lot like some African languages. And tell your friends we teach karate, too. That ought to bring some of them in." She looked at her watch. "Come on, let's go up front for a minute and watch the children leave. That's the school song they singing now."

> *We strong black brothers and sisters,*
> *Working in unity,*
> *We strong black brothers . . .*

The children were standing in a circle with Brother Juba, clasping hands, and they made room for Sister Shani and Doretha. Their faces and their voices were serious.

> *. . . and sisters,*
> *Building our community,*
> *We all work together, learn together*

Live in harmony,
We strong black brothers and sisters
Building for you and for me.

"Sister Shani?" Doretha said, as the children were
leaving. "I made up my mind. I want to join."

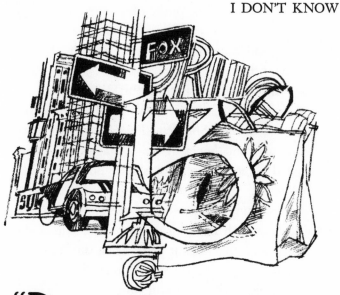

"Doretha, your sister's in another fight!"

Doretha didn't recognize the voice. And she didn't look around to see who had yelled. She was running too fast, out of her school cafeteria and over to the high school next door. She heard footsteps behind her and knew that other kids were running, too, but she didn't look back.

A crowd on the playground was roaring and moving as one, back and forth, as the fighters moved. Doretha heard a boy say, "Them girls bookin'!" and she started to yell.

"Alberta, Alberta! Let me through, let me get through!" By the time she pushed her way through the crowd, the two girls were on the ground. Doretha saw elbows and dungareed legs and a flash of long, bright green fingernails.

"Get off! Get off my sister, get off!"

She grabbed for the girl and an elbow sent her stumbling backward. She felt the pain as her back hit the ground and her arm scraped against a stone. She wanted to stay there, but she couldn't, she had to help Alberta.

The first thing she saw when she got up was the bloody strip of flesh hanging down on the side of Alberta's face and the hole it left. Then she saw the two men, a janitor and a teacher from the high school. One was helping Alberta up and the other was holding the girl back. Alberta's face was wet with tears and blood, and the look she gave Doretha was not defiant, but pleading.

"I'll drive her to the hospital," the janitor said. He took a clean handkerchief out of his back pocket, folded it quickly inside-out, and gave it to Alberta to hold against her cheek.

The other man gripped the girl's arm with a firm brown hand. "Come on, we're going to see the principal." He raised his voice. "Okay, now. Everybody back inside. Go back inside."

Doretha caught up with Alberta. "Can I go?" she asked the man. "I'm her sister."

He kept walking, but looked back over his shoulder. "You better get in touch with your parents and let them know what happened. I'm taking her to Freedmen's Hospital."

Doretha followed the green sedan down the street and watched it draw away from her and turn north at the corner. When she reached the intersection, she kept on across insead of turning. The skinned place on her arm hurt and she patted it.

She didn't know whether they would let her see her mother. She did know better than to phone. "Somebody's got to be dying before they call you to the phone," her mother had said. But maybe if she went there . . .

The laundry building was ugly. A large stone building with chipped orange paint. Customers never came there. The towels were delivered to them every day by truck drivers, who at the same time picked up the dirty towels and brought them back to the laundry.

The young man inside was black, and Doretha was glad. He was sitting at a small table, filing cards in a box.

"Hey, little sister," he said. A line of hair started under his bottom lip and met his small chin beard.

"Can I see Mrs. Freeman? It's real important."

"Sorry. Nobody can go back there." He nodded toward a closed door in the back. "You her daughter? Maybe I can tell her something for you."

"I got to tell her myself. Can't I see her for just a minute? Please? It won't take long."

"Well . . . wait a minute." He went to the bottom of the steps near the front door, and listened. Doretha heard a typewriter upstairs going slow motion. The man came back. "Okay, go ahead, but hurry up before the supervisor comes back down." He opened the door for her.

The large room was full of white machines, and tired-looking women in blue uniforms. Her mother was all the way across the room loading one of the machines. Doretha stepped around the piles of dirty towels that were scattered over the floor.

"Mama," she said.

Mrs. Freeman dropped the towels. "Sister! What's the matter?"

"Don't get upset, Mama, it's just . . ."

"Something's happened to Alberta!"

"She was in a fight, but . . ."

"Oh, Lord, is she dead?" She sagged against the machine.

"Mama, you not listening to me. Alberta's all right. The girl scratched her face, that's all. The janitor was taking her over to Freedmen's Hospital and he told me to tell you. But she's all right. She was walking and everything."

"Oh, thank God. I thought . . ." She straightened up slowly. "You know, Sister, I walk around all the time with this picture in my head of Alberta dead, dead in an alley, dead in a smashed-up car, gray-faced dead in a gray casket . . ."

"Mama, Alberta looked at me today, she looked at me, and I think she's going to be all right if we just . . ."

"No, Sister."

"But Mama . . ."

"No, Sister. I know you love Alberta and I love her, and we got to keep on doing everything we can for her, but we can't hope anymore. We got to live, too, and we can't live with our hearts going up and down on a yo-yo string."

"But she looked different, she was . . ."

"Why you patting your arm like that?"

Doretha turned her arm around so her mother could see. "I was trying to help Alberta," she said.

"Sister, are you crazy?" Her mother grabbed both

her shoulders and began to shake her. "Are you crazy? What's the matter with you, what's the matter with you?"

"M-M-Mama . . . Mama, she had real long fingernails. I had to help her."

"Not in a fight, Sister!" She pulled Doretha against her and held her tight. She leaned her face against her daughter's hair. "Sister, please . . ."

"Hey!" It was the man who had let Doretha in. He was beckoning from the doorway.

Mrs. Freeman patted the back of Doretha's head as if she couldn't let her go.

"Hey," the man said again.

"All right, honey, you got to go," Mrs. Freeman said. She let Doretha go. "You go on back to school now. We'll talk about it when I get home. And put something on that arm."

"Hurry up, little sister," the man said when she reached the door. "The typewriter's stopped."

She just had time to thank him.

When she got back to school, everybody was in the auditorium watching a film. Doretha sat in the back row to keep from walking by herself all the way to the front where seventh graders were supposed to sit. On the screen was a doctor with a blackboard and a long pointer.

"The symptoms of narcotics addiction," the doctor was saying, "usually manifest themselves . . ."

A boy down the row leaned over. "Hey, girl," he whispered. "Wasn't that your sister in the fight?"

"Uh-huh," Doretha said.

The two girls sitting between them turned to stare at her. One of them said, "Is it true? Is it true she got both her eyes scratched out?"

The boy was excited. "I heard this dude found one of her eyeballs on the basketball court and took it to the nurse," he said.

They were leaning up and staring at her, greedy for bad news. "No," she said. "She had a scratch on her face, that's all."

They were disappointed. They sat back and turned to the screen.

Doretha closed her eyes. On the screen of her eyelids, she saw herself. Stepping over Alberta's eyeballs to follow her. Down the grassless hill toward a blinding white light. Moving when Alberta moved. Moving toward—she didn't know. *Come back, Alberta.* Behind the light—she didn't know. *Alberta, come back.* Home. She wanted to go home. She couldn't go home. Alberta was pulling her. Down the grassless, flowerless, airless, loveless hill, down the . . . *Albertaaa! Come baaack!* Pulling her into the blinding . . . *Albertaaa!*

Albertaaaaaa! Albertaaaaaaaaaaaa! Dragging her into the light. The light! The light!

The lights were on in the auditorium when she opened her eyes.

" . . . classroom discussions tomorrow on the film," Mr. Hicks, the principal, was saying. "It's a little after three now, so go quietly to your lockers, and you're dismissed."

Doretha didn't go to her locker. Forget the homework. She wanted to get home before anybody else could ask her about the fight.

When she got home, Alberta was coming downstairs with a shopping bag. A white patch covered the whole side of her face. Doretha saw the clothes in the bag.

"Where you going?" she asked.

"Out."

"Out where?"

"Just out," Alberta said. "Different places. Wherever Renee's car goes."

"Don't go. Stay here with me and Mama."

"What for, Sister? What I want to stay here for? You know what I do when I go out?" She set the bag down. "I laugh, that's what I do."

"We laugh, too, Alberta."

"You don't understand, Sister. I mean I laugh all

the time. At everything. Even if it's not funny. As long as it's not happening to me. You *dig*? And I don't fail classes, and I don't care about money, and I don't get lonesome, and don't nobody hurt my feelings, 'cause I'm too busy laughing and having fun. So you might as well shut up. I'm going." She picked up the bag again.

"No, Alberta," Doretha begged. She grabbed the handles of the shopping bag and tried to pull it from her sister.

"Let go, Sister."

"No, Alberta, don't go. Please don't go."

"Let go!" Alberta snatched the bag away. "I don't want to be here when Mama comes."

"You mean you don't want to see her cry," Doretha said. Her voice was getting louder and louder. "*I* got to tell her you gone, and *I* got to watch her face crunch all up. While you laughing and having fun." And then she was yelling. "You don't have to go, Alberta. You can stay here and laugh. I know something real funny you can laugh at. YOU CAN LAUGH AT MAMA CRYING."

Alberta walked away, slow, slow, loose. She got a sweater from the closet, pushed it down in the bag, and left.

Doretha stood in the middle of the front room,

feeling it get smaller and smaller. All of a sudden she wanted to run behind Alberta and yell, "Take me with you! Take me with you!" All of a sudden, more than anything, she wanted to be in Renee's car. Going to a fun place. Acting crazy and laughing. Laughing loud at anything, at everything. As long as it wasn't happening to her.

Three days later Alberta was back, looking sad and tired.

ME, AGE 13. TREE-WALLS, SKY-ROOF, LONNIE—LOVE

Screams. Four dashikis flashing. Drums beating. Lonnie! Lonnie at the mike...

Doretha closed her book. She had seen herself.

She had seen others, too. Her father and her mother, Grandpa Jack, and all the others. But most of all, she had seen herself. And her strength that came from their strength. Even Alberta, who didn't understand yet, had once loved her and helped to make her strong. And even Coley.

In a way, her Doretha Book was a book of hard times. And she never wanted to forget them, the hard colors of her life. Going through her book and thinking about them all together like that, she saw that she could beat them. Fight them and laugh at them, like Grandpa said.

But what she would remember most were the good times, the family and friend times, the love times, that rainbowed their way through the hard times. She would remember them over and over, and look for more.

She laid her book on the floor beside the bed. "I'm me," she said. "I'm not Alberta, I'm me."

She had lost the bet she had made with herself when she opened her book. Alberta still wasn't home. But she was going to sleep, now, and whatever night her sister did come home would be the night she would start showing her what she had seen. Not all at once, but a little at a time.

After she closed her eyes, Doretha remembered her flute. Maybe she would take it with her to Sister

Shani's school the next time she went. She couldn't really play it, and she didn't know why she wanted to take it.

It was just a feeling she had.

About the Author

Born in Parmele, North Carolina, Eloise Greenfield grew up in Washington, D.C., where she lives now with her husband and family. She is the mother of a grown son and a teen-age daughter. As a youngster, she studied piano, sang with three friends in a group called the Langston Harmonettes, and won a citywide typing contest when she was fourteen. But not until she was twenty-two, after attending Miner Teachers College, did she begin to write. During her years of working in government offices and raising her family, Ms. Greenfield continued writing, and her sensitive short stories and articles were published in magazines. Her first book for children, a picture book called *Bubbles,* was published in 1972; her Crowell Biography *Rosa Parks* was published in 1973. As an active member of the D.C. Black Writers Workshop, she has been a leader in both the adult fiction and children's literature divisions.

About *Sister,* Ms. Greenfield says, "I wanted to tell my young Brothers and Sisters not to ever forget the strength they have inherited."

133680

DATE DUE

OCT 2 9 2001			
OCT 2 9 2001			
JUL 2 0 04			

J G
Greenfield, Eloise.
Sister